THE STORY OF THE
SAN ANTONIO
SPURS

CREATIVE EDUCATION

Published by Creative Education
123 South Broad Street
Mankato, Minnesota 56001
Creative Education is an imprint of The Creative Company.

DESIGN AND PRODUCTION BY **EVANSDAY DESIGN**

PHOTOGRAPHS BY Associated Press, AP, Getty Images (Brian Bahr,
Bill Baptist / NBAE, Andrew D. Bernstein / NBAE, Chris Birck / NBAE,
Nathaniel S. Butler / NBAE, Focus on Sport, Rodolfo Gonzalez /
Stringer, Otto Greule Jr. / Allsport, JEFF HAYNES / AFP, Andy Hayt /
NBAE, Ron Hoskins / NBAE, Ronald Martinez / Allsport, NBA Photo
Library / NBAE, Joel Sartore / National Geographic, Gregory
Shamus / NBAE, Jon SooHoo / NBAE)

LIBRARY OF CONGRESS CATALOGING-IN-PUBLICATION DATA

LeBoutillier, Nate.
The story of the San Antonio Spurs / by Nate LeBoutillier.
p. cm. — (The NBA—a history of hoops)
Includes index.
ISBN-13: 978-1-58341-424-8
1. San Antonio Spurs (Basketball team)—History—
Juvenile literature. I. Title. II. Series.

GV885.52.S26L43 2006
796.32'36409764351—dc22   2005051767

9 8 7 6 5 4 3

COVER PHOTO: *Tim Duncan*

THE STORY OF THE
SAN ANTONIO
SPURS

NATE LeBOUTILLIER

CREATIVE EDUCATION

Texas is big.

AND THE BEST PLAYERS FOR THE SAN ANTONIO SPURS—
ONE OF TEXAS'S THREE PROFESSIONAL BASKETBALL
TEAMS—HAVE ALWAYS BEEN THE SAME. FROM 6-FOOT-8
FORWARD GEORGE GERVIN TO 7-FOOT-2 CENTER ARTIS
GILMORE TO 7-FOOT CENTER DAVID ROBINSON, LARGE
HAS BEEN IN CHARGE. IT WAS A PERFECT FIT, THEN, WHEN
7-FOOT TIM DUNCAN STROLLED ONTO THE COURT IN 1997.
DUNCAN, A WORKHORSE CENTER, DID WHAT A BIG MAN
SHOULD: HE BLOCKED SHOTS, GRABBED REBOUNDS,
MUSCLED FOR POSITION, SCORED POINTS, AND THREW
HIS WEIGHT AROUND WHEN HE HAD TO. THE RESULT FOR
SAN ANTONIO? CHAMPIONSHIP BASKETBALL.

SAN ANTONIO SPURS
San Antonio Texas

RAISED TO FIGHT

1

SAN ANTONIO, TEXAS, IS ONE OF AMERICA'S MOST historic cities. Shortly after Spanish missionaries founded it, San Antonio came under Mexican control. In 1836, 184 Texans fought off nearly 5,000 Mexican soldiers at a mission called the Alamo for two weeks before the Mexicans prevailed and killed the defenders. Despite the outcome of that battle, Texas did eventually earn its independence. More than a century later, a National Basketball Association (NBA) team moved to the "Alamo City." That team, named the San Antonio Spurs, quickly earned a reputation for its fighting spirit as well.

The Spurs franchise was founded in 1967 and named the Dallas Chaparrals. One of the original teams in the American Basketball Association (ABA), the Chaps were led in their first two seasons by such fine players as

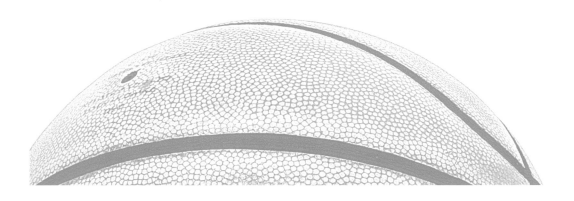

SPURS

Averaging 19 points a game over his three seasons in Dallas, Cincinnatus Powell was an ABA All-Star

10

A four-time NBA scoring champion, George Gervin made even the most impossible shots look simple

forward Cincinnatus Powell, center John Beasley, and swingman Cliff Hagan, who also served as the team's coach. But sometimes fewer than 500 people attended home games. Even after the team's owners changed the club's name to the Texas Chaparrals and played home games in Fort Worth and Lubbock in an attempt to gain statewide fan support, attendance remained low.

Finally, in 1973, the Chaps were sold to Texas millionaire Red McCombs, who moved the team to San Antonio and renamed it the Spurs. "We made a few key deals, won some games, and suddenly we were drawing a crowd," said Spurs general manager John Begnoz. "We were stunned. People figured we were geniuses, but we didn't even know what we were doing."

What the Spurs did was acquire two talented players—towering center Swen Nater and forward George Gervin—from the struggling Virginia Squires franchise early in the 1973–74 season. Gervin, who joined the Spurs at the age of 20, never seemed rattled or overly excited on the court. He was so cool that teammates had nicknamed him "The Iceman."

THE ICEMAN'S FINGER ROLL

It was the sweetest of shots: the finger roll a la George "The Iceman" Gervin. Floating toward the rim, Gervin would flick the ball underhanded, and it would arc like a beautiful rainbow before swishing into the net. When asked how he perfected the finger roll, Gervin replied, "I got tired of dunking. I got tired of hitting my wrist. The finger roll was smoother and looked better, and it was easy for me to do with my long arms. But I took it from Wilt [Chamberlain], Connie Hawkins, and Dr. J [Julius Erving] and added it to my game." Gervin spent 12 seasons with San Antonio, bringing his unique art to the basketball court. By 2006, he remained San Antonio's career leader in many categories, including points, games played—and finger rolls.

THE ICEMAN

THE ICEMAN WAS AN INSTANT STAR IN SAN ANTONIO. In his first full season, he led the team in scoring with 23 points per game, many of them via his famed "finger roll." With Gervin leading the way, the Spurs went 51–33 in 1974–75 and 50–34 the next season. San Antonio was a success, but the ABA was struggling. So, in 1976, the Spurs joined the NBA, and the ABA was dissolved.

The Spurs made the playoffs in their first NBA season. Then, in 1977–78, Gervin led the league in scoring with 27 points per game. The Spurs flew high that season and the next, winning their division each time. In 1979, center Billy Paultz and forward Larry Kenon helped lead the team all the way to the Eastern Conference Finals, with Gervin playing a starring role. "I consider the game won when Ice has his hands on the ball," said Paultz.

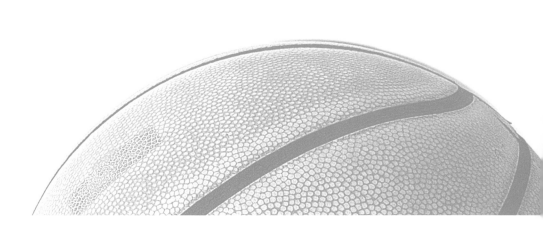

13

SPURS

Although best-known for his offense, Larry Kenon made NBA history with 11 steals in one 1976 game

Center Artis Gilmore was a gentle giant off the court but a frightening force when going to the basket

In 1980, the Spurs brought in new coach Stan Albeck, yet fell short of the NBA Finals in both 1981 and 1982. San Antonio then traded for 7-foot-2 center Artis Gilmore, one of the NBA's biggest players. "[More than his sheer size] was the way he intimidated people—the way opposing players came to the middle, saw him, and traveled or threw the ball away," Chicago Bulls coach Jerry Sloan said of Gilmore. "Those are things that mean more than points."

With Gilmore providing the muscle and forwards Mike Mitchell and Gervin spearheading the offense, the Spurs won a team-record 53 games in 1982–83. In the playoffs, they advanced as far as the Western Conference Finals before falling to the Los Angeles Lakers. The Spurs then went into a tailspin. In 1984, they missed the playoffs for the first time in their NBA history. A year later, San Antonio decided to rebuild and traded Gervin to the Chicago Bulls.

Young guard Alvin Robertson was called on to fill the void. "The Spurs were always known as a high-scoring offensive team led by Ice," said new San Antonio coach Cotton Fitzsimmons. "But we needed toughness and quickness. Alvin gave us that look." Robertson was named an All-Star and the league's Defensive Player of the Year in 1985–86. Still, San Antonio struggled that year and the next.

Opposing ball handlers used extra caution around Alvin Robertson, the top ball thief of the late '80s

THE MAN CALLED POP

When the NBA named Gregg Popovich the Coach of the Year after the 2002–03 season, it capped off a list of impressive and unlikely accomplishments. Popovich earned a social studies degree and played basketball at the United States Air Force Academy in the late 1960s. He then spent time serving in the military, earning his Master's Degree, and coaching and teaching at a small college in California throughout the 1970s and much of the '80s. In 1988, he joined the Spurs as an assistant coach, taking over as head coach in May 1996. When asked why Coach "Pop" and his team are so successful, Doug Moe, a former NBA coach, replied simply, "He's smart. They play smart." Considering Popovich's academic resume, "smart" seems the right word.

THE SPURS WELCOME "THE ADMIRAL"

SAN ANTONIO'S POOR RECORD GAVE THE TEAM THE top overall pick in the 1987 NBA Draft. With it, the Spurs selected David Robinson, a 7-foot-1 center from the United States Naval Academy. Even though Robinson would be obligated to serve in the armed forces after graduation, the Spurs knew he was worth the wait. In the meantime, the Spurs posted losing records in both 1987–88 and 1988–89.

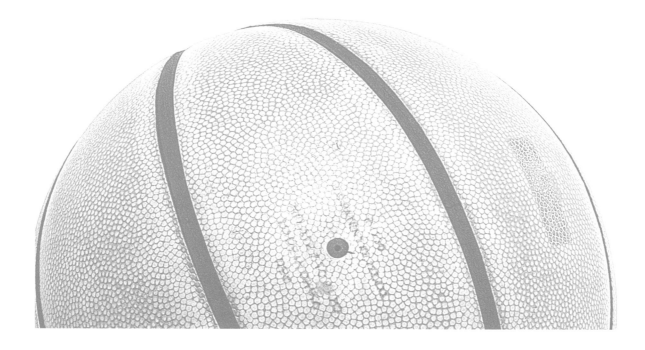

19

A 10-time All-Star, David Robinson was one of the fastest and most graceful centers in basketball history

SPURS

Dennis Rodman and David Robinson made for a strange but successful combination in the mid-1990s

In 1989, Robinson was released from his naval duties and joined the team, which also drafted talented forward Sean Elliot from the University of Arizona. Robinson, nicknamed "The Admiral" because of his navy background, used his remarkable agility to become an instant star, scoring 24 points a game as the Spurs surged to a 56–26 record in 1989–90. "He has the talent all us big guys only hope and dream for," said Spurs backup center Caldwell Jones. "No other big guy I've ever seen is anywhere near as quick and fast as he is."

Over the next two seasons, Robinson grew more dominant and Elliot emerged as a versatile contributor. The Spurs made the playoffs both seasons but fell short of a championship. Some accused the team's leaders—particularly the easy-going Robinson—of lacking the "killer instinct" needed to win tough playoff games. In 1993, San Antonio made a move to bring some fire to the lineup, trading Elliot to the Detroit Pistons for intense forward Dennis Rodman.

COURAGEOUS COMEBACK

When Spurs forward Sean Elliot's kidney gave out in 1999 after a six-year battle with a progressive kidney disease, many thought it spelled the end of his basketball career. "I was a healthy young man, and I thought I was invincible before I was diagnosed with kidney disease," said Elliott, an NBA All-Star in 1992–93 and 1995–96. Elliot's brother Noel donated one of his own kidneys to Sean for a transplant operation, and Elliot took back both his life and his place in the Spurs' lineup. After recovering from the transplant, he came back to play during the 1999–00 and 2000–01 seasons. Even while sick with kidney disease, he managed to start all 50 games in 1998–99, averaging 11.2 points per game to help the Spurs win their first NBA title.

Robinson and Rodman could not have been more different. Robinson was one of the league's most straight-laced players; Rodman was covered with tattoos and dyed his hair wild colors. Robinson was known for his graceful style and offensive skills; Rodman was known for his scrappy style and defensive skills. About the only thing the two had in common was their desire to win.

In 1993–94, Robinson scored nearly 30 points per game, and Rodman grabbed 17 boards per game as the teammates led the NBA in both categories. The next season, Robinson was named the NBA's Most Valuable Player (MVP), and the Spurs went 62–20, driving as far as the Western Conference Finals, but San Antonio decided to make a change after the team lost the series. Frustrated by Rodman's odd and often disruptive behavior, the team traded him to Chicago.

In 1995, the Spurs brought Elliot back after he had spent just one season in Detroit and did the same with point guard Avery Johnson, who had spent a year with Golden State after three seasons in San Antonio. But, once again, they fell flat in the playoffs.

23

SPURS

Hustling guard Avery Johnson's strong leadership made him an NBA coach after his playing days

4

IN 1996, SPURS GENERAL MANAGER GREGG POPOVICH moved to the bench as the team's new coach. Popovich proved to be a popular leader, but injuries to Robinson, Elliot, and forward Chuck Person led to a disastrous 20–62 mark—the worst record in franchise history. Because of their horrible season, the Spurs were given the top overall pick in the 1997 NBA Draft, and they used it to select center Tim Duncan from Wake Forest University.

Like Robinson, the 7-foot and 260-pound Duncan was extremely agile and relied on superb fundamental skills. The rookie became an instant All-Star. "Once he gets more comfortable, he's going to be unbelievable," said Robinson. "He can score on the block, he's got great post moves, and he's a great passer."

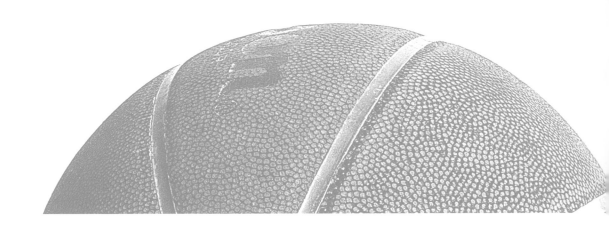

25

SPURS

Tim Duncan was an outstanding competitive swimmer as a teenager before turning his focus to hoops

Mario Elie helped bring three NBA championships to Texas—two to Houston and one to San Antonio

With Duncan added to the mix, San Antonio leaped to 56–26 in 1997–98. The next season, the Spurs were virtually unstoppable. Robinson, Duncan, and backup 7-footer Will Perdue formed a daunting frontcourt, and Elliot and guard Mario Elie provided consistent outside firepower with the speedy Johnson serving as floor general.

Coach Popovich guided this talented lineup to a league-best 37–13 record. Then, in the 1999 playoffs, the Spurs destroyed the Timberwolves, Lakers, Trail Blazers, and Knicks to capture their first NBA championship. "Defense won it for us," said Robinson. "This championship sends a message that persistence and hard work can pay off."

Three competitive but unfulfilling seasons followed before the Spurs moved into a new arena, the SBC Center, at the beginning of the 2002–03 season. Once resettled, Duncan (who averaged 23.3 points, 12.9 rebounds, and 2.9 blocks per game) won his second NBA MVP award, and the Spurs captured another NBA championship, topping the New Jersey Nets in the 2003 Finals. The title took on special significance as it sent Robinson into retirement on top. Robinson finished his career as just the 12th NBA player to score more than 20,000 points and collect 10,000 rebounds.

HORRY IN THE CLUTCH

With six NBA championship rings, forward Robert Horry can be proud. But the fact that he won them playing for three different teams—the Houston Rockets (1994 and 1995), the Los Angeles Lakers (2000, 2001, and 2002), and the San Antonio Spurs (2005)—made him only the second player (after forward John Salley) in NBA history to do so. Although never a regular-season star, Horry earned a reputation as a lucky charm, largely due to his clutch shot-making; he won Game 5 of the 2005 NBA Finals for the Spurs on a buzzer-beating three-pointer. As sportswriter Marc Stein put it: "No one as far down the star scale as Horry has been this steely cool and clutch in playoff crunch time for so long and so often and in so many different uniforms."

Two young guards, Tony Parker and Manu Ginobili, replaced Robinson as fan favorites. Thanks to their hustle and smarts—and, of course, the fine play of Duncan—the Spurs found themselves in the NBA Finals once again in 2005. In an exciting seven-game battle with the defending champion Detroit Pistons, San Antonio pulled out Game 7 in front of its home crowd for its third championship in seven years. "You follow your leader," said Parker of Duncan, who was named Finals MVP. "Timmy is the leader of the team, and he just carried us tonight."

From The Iceman to The Admiral to Tim Duncan, the Spurs have featured some of the NBA's finest big men. With year-in and year-out excellence and three championships to show for their effort, these players and more have given San Antonio a team that never backs down, making it a natural fit in the Alamo City.

29

SPURS

Guard Manu Ginobili led his homeland of Argentina to the Olympic gold medal in basketball in 2004.

THE FOREIGN GUARD The Spurs searched the world over for the best players, and they found two in France and Argentina. Point guard Tony Parker, the son of a basketball player and model, hailed from Paris, France. Possibly the fastest player in the NBA, he got his start with the Spurs as a 19-year-old in 2001. Manu Ginobili was a national hero, a celebrity of god-like proportions in Argentina. For the Spurs, he became invaluable upon his arrival in 2003. Improving by the minute, Ginobili earned NBA All-Star status in 2004–05. "He's been in a lot of big games in both the NBA and overseas for years even though he's a young guy," said Spurs coach Gregg Popovich of Ginobili. "He doesn't feel pressure, he relishes it." Popovich could have been talking about either of his guards.

SPURS

Speedy point guard Tony Parker helped power the Spurs to the 2005 NBA title and a 2006 playoff run

INDEX